INTRODUCTION

The combat tank is perhaps the most feared of all land weapons. Crunching everything in their path, these huge vehicles thunder across the roughest ground. Their guns can destroy enemy targets that are several kilometres away.

● M1A2

Machine gun; revolves 265 degrees

Antenna; keeps the tank in radio contact

Caterpillar tracks; can cross any terrain

JOB DONE!

A tank shell explodes with a flash of light. Another target is destroyed. The tank rumbles away across the landscape.

▲ The Abrams M1A2 can fire different kinds of missiles from its huge main gun. Armour-piercing shells can destroy another tank from over 3.2 km (2 miles) away.

CATERPILLAR TRACKS: Metal plates joined in a continuous loop.

CONTENTS

ULTIMATE MILITARY MACHINES

TANKS

Tim Cooke

WAYLAND

www.waylandbooks.co.uk

Published in paperback in Great Britain in 2018
by Wayland

Copyright © 2014 Brown Bear Books Ltd.

Wayland
An imprint of Hachette Children's Group
Part of Hodder & Stoughton
Carmelite House
50 Victoria Embankment
London EC4Y 0DZ
An Hachette UK Company
www.hachette.co.uk
www.hachettechildrens.co.uk

All Rights Reserved.

Dewey Number: 623.7'4752-dc23
ISBN: 978 1 5263 0727 9
10 9 8 7 6 5 4 3 2 1

Brown Bear Books Ltd.
First Floor
9–17 St. Albans Place
London
N1 0NX

Managing Editor: Tim Cooke
Picture Manager: Sophie Mortimer
Art Director: Jeni Child
Editorial Director: Lindsey Lowe
Children's Publisher: Anne O'Daly
Production Consultant: Alastair Gourlay

Printed in China

A NEW WEAPON

In World War I (1914–1918), guns with wheels sank into the muddy battlefields. The British invented a weapon that used caterpillar tracks to cross difficult terrain. With its metal armour and mounted guns, the new tank terrified the enemy.

▲ 'Tank' was a codename used to disguise the new invention. It stuck!

THE AFV

A tank is one sort of AFV, which means 'armoured fighting vehicle'. An AFV is a vehicle that moves with its own power, has protective armour and is fitted with guns or cannon.

● M60

A 105 mm M68 cannon is the main gun.

▲ The M60 medium tank was made in the United States. Today it is used by three countries.

CANNON: A powerful gun that fires heavy shells.

WHAT IS A TANK?

A tank is a tracked, armoured fighting vehicle designed to destroy enemy targets on the battlefield. Although they are big, tanks are mobile and well armed. They can defend themselves as well as attacking the enemy.

ARIETE

Large, angular turret with sloping front

Box-shaped hull; streamlined with flat surfaces

SPECIFICATIONS
Weight: 54 tonnes (59½ tons)
Crew: 4
Length: 9.67 m (31¾ feet)
Main armament: 120 mm smoothbore gun
Speed: 65 km/h (40 mph)

BATTLE TANK

The Ariete main battle tank is made in Italy. The firing system for the primary gun is fully computerised. It helps the tank to fire at moving targets.

MAIN BATTLE TANK: A tank that is heavy, but still highly mobile.

"In many situations that seemed desperate, the tank has been a most vital factor..."
GENERAL DOUGLAS MACARTHUR

THE ABRAMS

The Abrams is the main battle tank of the U.S. Army and U.S. Marine Corps. It can operate in any weather, in the daytime or at night. The Abrams is very powerful. It could destroy any other armoured fighting vehicle in the world.

SPECIFICATIONS

Weight: 62 tonnes (68½ tons)
Length: 9.77 m (32 feet)
Crew: 4
Main armament: 120 mm cannon
Speed: 67.5 km/h (42 mph)

Heavy machine gun on the tank commander's hatch

Long main gun

Extra storage space on the turret's rear

Machine gun at side of main gun

What is NOT A TANK

Self-propelled guns (top), wheeled armoured vehicles (centre), and reconnaissance vehicles (bottom) are not tanks.

M109

PIRANHA

FOX

TURRET: The top section of a tank; it can turn in all directions.

TANK MISSION

Tanks have all sorts of jobs. Often, they are used to clear the way for ground troops to advance. They can speed through enemy territory at up to 40 km/h (25 mph). Amphibious tanks are used for landings from the sea.

LAND TO SEA

The advanced amphibious assault vehicle (AAAV) travels through water and then drives onto the shore. It carries an attacking force of up to 18 Marines.

▼ The AAAV can travel in water by using high-speed water jets.

● AAAV

30 mm main gun

Water pours quickly off the hull

AMPHIBIOUS: A vehicle that works on land and in water.

Tank opening a temporary folding bridge

▲ Tanks do all sorts of jobs. In World War I, they carried wood to fill enemy trenches (above) so the infantry could cross.

TANK BATTLES

There were several tank battles in World War II. The biggest were at El Alamein in Egypt, in France after 'D-Day' and at Kursk in Russia. At El Alamein, the German Afrika Korps used Panzer III tanks.

FAST AND DEADLY

In World War II, the German Army was expert at using tanks. The tanks were small, but quick and powerful. They were vital to the tactic of Blitzkrieg, or 'lightning war'. At the start of the war, German armoured forces sped across Europe. Their advance was so quick that their enemies were overwhelmed.

▲ German Panzer III tanks cross the North African desert.

BLITZKRIEG: A German tactic that relied on rapid advances by tanks.

TANK SIZES

Tanks are classed by size: light, medium or heavy. Thanks to technology, tanks have become lighter and easier to manoeuvre, but they are still very strong.

HEAVY TANK

The German Leopard 2A6 has super-strong armour. It is made by mixing ceramic with metal.

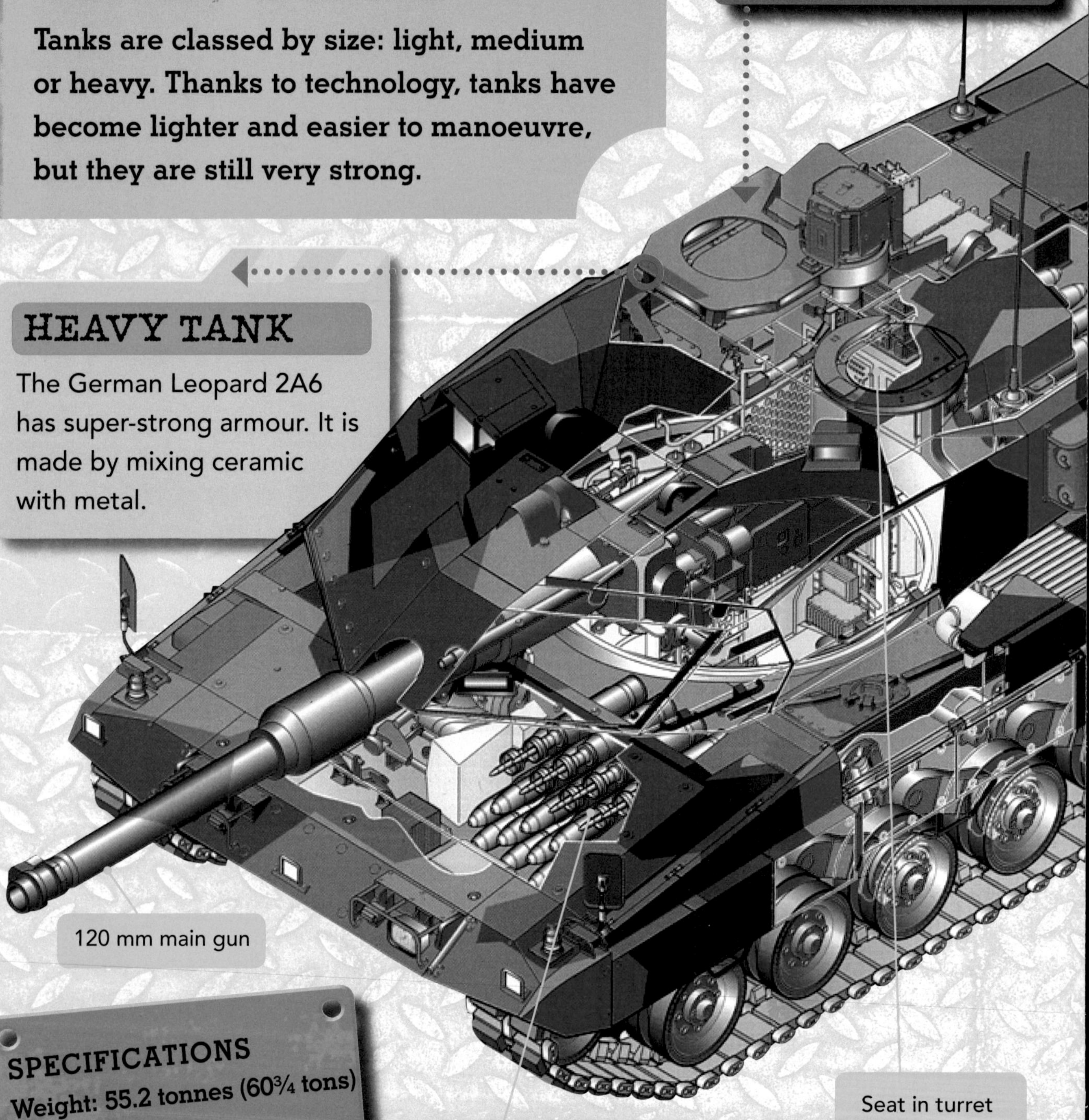

120 mm main gun

SPECIFICATIONS

Weight: 55.2 tonnes (60¾ tons)

Crew: 4

Length: 9.67 m (31¾ feet)

Main armament: 120 mm smoothbore cannon

Shells for main gun; the tank carries 42 rounds

Seat in turret for tank commander

CERAMIC: A strong modern material based on fired clay.

Cooling fan
for engine

SPECIFICATIONS
Weight: 22.6 tonnes (25 tons)
Crew: 4
Length: 9.3 m (30½ feet)
Main armament: 105 mm
    rifled gun

LIGHT TANKS

The Stingray was a U.S. light tank. Light tanks are fast, but their armour is not very heavy or strong. It might not withstand a direct hit!

ELECTRONICS

The Abrams M1A2 has high-tech electronic systems for good communication and for locating the enemy.

MAIN BATTLE TANKS

Tanks that combine the armour of a heavy tank and the speed and firepower of a medium tank are called main battle tanks (MBTs).

M1A2

FIREPOWER

AFVs are machines designed for carrying weapons. They can be armed with machine guns, smoothbore or rifled cannon, rockets and even anti-aircraft missiles.

M1 ABRAMS

GUN GALLERY

Tank guns can be fired on the move, at night or in any kind of weather conditions. Technology has made guns compact and lightweight, but also more powerful and able to fire further than ever before.

MAIN GUN

The tank's turret swings around so that the main gun can be fired in any direction. Tank cannon can fire different kinds of ammunition, such as high-explosive or armour-piercing shells.

▶ Tracer shells are coated with chemicals that glow to show their path in the dark.

RIFLED CANNON: A gun with grooves inside the barrel to spin a shell.

STRYKER

Slat armour to protect against projectiles

Remote weapons station

Wheels with non-flammable tyres

▲ The Stryker is an AFV used to carry soldiers. Its remote weapons station can hold a .50 calibre machine gun or anti-tank missiles, as here.

IN THE DARK

Warfare does not stop at night. In modern tanks, infrared technology finds the target and pinpoints it using lasers.

TANK KILLER

The tank's biggest enemy is the anti-tank guided missile (ATGM). Fired from a distance, the missile locks on to its target. It can destroy a light or medium tank.

INFRARED: A system that 'sees' objects by the radiation they give off.

OTHER WEAPONS

AFVs have more weapons in addition to their main guns. They can use a range of machine guns and other cannon, depending on the target. Many of the weapons can be fitted to different families of AFVs.

BRADLEY M3

Hull of aluminium and steel armour

Chamber holds three crewmembers and two scouts

Hatch door at rear

25 mm Bushmaster chain gun

SPECIFICATIONS

Weight: 27.6 tonnes (30½ tons)

Crew: 3

Length: 6.5 m (21½ feet)

Main armament: 25 mm chain gun

Speed: 66 km/h (41 mph)

"The Bradley's TOW missile system was lethal at long ranges against all forms of enemy armour." U.S. OFFICIAL REPORT ON THE GULF WAR

DESTROYER

The Bradley M3 has a 25 mm chain gun and a sight unit that magnifies the target. In the Gulf War (1990–1991), Bradleys destroyed more Iraqi tanks than the Abrams tanks did.

TOW: Tube-launched, optically-tracked, wire-guided missile.

WALL OF SMOKE

Many AFVs carry smoke grenades. They fire the grenades to create a smokescreen that hides the tank as it gets ready for action.

MLRS

The MLRS – multiple launch rocket system – can fire 12 rockets together or individually, or in waves of 2 to 12. The MLRS is built on a similar chassis to the Bradley tanks.

▼ An MLRS opens fire in the desert during the Gulf War in Iraq in 1991. The MLRS was nicknamed 'Steel Rain'.

CHASSIS: The base of a vehicle that is attached to the wheels or tracks.

LOOK INSIDE A TANK

Modern main battle tanks have a crew of three or four. Although a tank looks large from the outside, its hull and turret have to hold the crew, the weapons, the ammunition and the engine. There are also the navigations, sighting and fire control systems. This means that there is little space to spare, so the crew has to operate in cramped conditions.

Remote weapons station allows commander to stay in turret

Tough armour for protection

DRIVING A TANK

The driver sits in the front of the tank, steering the vehicle. The other members of the crew are the commander, gunner and loader. They sit in the turret. Their job is to load, aim and fire the main gun. The commander can also drive the tank if required.

Plastic, nylon and ceramic materials in place of steel

FIRE CONTROL SYSTEM: Keeps the main gun locked on its target.

ABRAMS

Ammunition for main gun

Armoured side skirts

▶ This is where the tank's gunner sits. He targets the enemy and fires the main gun. He has a thermal imaging sight to find targets in the dark.

THERMAL IMAGING: Making a picture from the heat something gives off.

COMMAND AND TRAINING

U.S. tank operators train at the U.S. Army Armour Centre in Fort Benning, Georgia. They do not have to spend much time inside tanks. They spend hour after hour in AFV simulators, which re-create the different situations that tankers might face in battle.

Storage in the rear

BENNING

"[Fort Benning] is the best facility for instruction I've seen anywhere in the world, bar none."
MAJOR GENERAL ROBERT BROWN, U.S. ARMY

TRAINING

All tank recruits in the U.S. Army have already done basic combat training. They do special courses in AFV mechanics and tactics. Tankers use computer simulation to learn how to manoeuvre and fire.

TANKER: A member of a tank crew.

Commander mans turret machine gun

Letters identify nationality of tank

SPACE

You need space for tank practice. NATO troops learn live firing and tank tactics at a special training ground in Suffield, Alberta, a remote and empty part of Canada.

▶ A gunner trains in an Abrams M1 tank simulator at the Armour Centre at Fort Benning.

WAR GAMES

Computer simulators help tankers to practise driving, firing and tactics. A tank simulator is one of the most advanced video games in the world – and one day it might help save the tanker's life.

TACTICS: How troops and weapons are used together in warfare.

19

TANK HISTORY

Since it first appeared on the muddy battlefields of World War I (1914–1918), the tank has been a key feature of all military campaigns on land.

WORLD WAR I

At Cambrai, France, in November 1917, 300 British tanks pushed 6.4 km (4 miles) into enemy territory. It was a turning point in armoured warfare.

"We heard strange throbbing noises. Lumbering slowly towards us were three mechanical monsters such as we had never seen before."
BERT CHANEY, BRITISH INFANTRY, WORLD WAR I

▲ British tanks rolled over the mud and trenches of the Western Front without getting stuck.

INFANTRY: Soldiers who fight on foot.

ARGONNE

The U.S. Army used Renault tanks at the Battle of the Argonne Forest, in France, in 1918. The tanks helped to force the Germans into a position where they decided to surrender.

Compartment holds two-man crew

Machine gun in turret

WORLD WAR II

The rolling plains of Kursk, in Russia, were the location of history's biggest tank battle. It took place during World War II (1939–1945). In July 1943, German leader Adolf Hitler sent 1,800 tanks to fight a much larger Soviet force of 3,600 tanks and armoured vehicles.

KURSK

The battle took place over 10 days of intense fighting. The Germans could not break through the Soviet defences. The Soviets held off the German attack. They won a strategic victory.

STRATEGIC: Related to the overall plan for a campaign or war.

WORLD WAR II

World War II tanks helped break enemy lines and protected infantry during the fighting. They blasted through any obstacles in the way of an advance. They also fought other tanks. Two remarkable tanks from the war were the Soviet T-34 and the American M4 Sherman.

ACE

Germany's top-scoring tank ace was Michael Wittmann (above, standing, hands on hips, with his Tiger tank crew in Normandy).

SOVIET T-34

Many people think the T-34 was the best tank of World War II. It was based on a U.S. design, but was tougher than many other tanks. That was because it was built to withstand the harsh Russian winter.

"The finest tank in the world."
FIELD MARSHAL PAUL VON KLEIST ON THE T-34.

SOVIET T-34

Wide tracks for better traction

Driver's hatch

TRACTION: The amount of grip that pulls a vehicle along.

SHERMAN

The U.S. M4 Sherman was an outstanding medium tank. More than 48,000 Shermans were made. The British variant was the Sherman Firefly. Its turret was adapted to accommodate a 17-pounder gun.

17-pounder gun

Each Sherman tank had 4,537 parts

Digging tools

"If you got hit ... you had to get out of there as quickly as possible."
MARTIN GOLDSTEIN,
M4 SHERMAN TANK DRIVER

TIGER: A German heavy tank developed in 1942 to fight Allied AFVs.

WAR IN THE DESERT

Deserts are ideal terrain for AFVs. In October 1973, tanks led a surprise attack by Syria and Egypt on Israel. Israeli tanks led the defence against the Arab attack.

• CENTURION

BORDER CLASH

Syrian tanks attacked the Golan Heights, between Syria and Israel. Egyptian tanks rolled into the Sinai Desert. In just three weeks of fighting, the Arab countries lost about 2,300 tanks; the Israelis lost only 400.

▶ An Israeli F-4 Phantom flies above an Israeli Centurion tank.

"I looked through the binoculars and saw a sight I will never forget: hundreds of Syrian tanks on the Golan."
EFFI EITAM, ISRAELI ARMY

GOLAN HEIGHTS: A high, flat area on the border of Syria and Israel.

M1 SMOKESCREEN

WAR IN IRAQ

In 1990, Iraqi dictator Saddam Hussein invaded Kuwait. An international Coalition went to war to stop him. Ground and air attacks wiped out almost all of Iraq's armoured units in six weeks. The Coalition destroyed 4,000 tanks and lost just four.

"The battle [in the streets of Baghdad] set new standards for the use of armour in urban combat."
CAPTAIN JASON CONROY, IRAQ, APRIL 2003

INTO AFGHANISTAN

After deadly attacks on America on 11 September 2001, the United States and its allies went to war in Afghanistan. They faced Taliban and al-Qaeda units. The Alliance quickly destroyed the enemy's old tanks.

◀ A Dutch M1 surges through the desert in Helmand, Afghanistan. Dutch tanks supported U.S. efforts to clear the Taliban from the area.

COALITION: A temporary alliance of people or countries.

GALLERY

There are many types of AFVs in use today. AFVs are expensive vehicles, so countries sometimes work together to design and build them. This gallery features some of the outstanding tanks and other AFVs from around the world today.

M109

The M109A6 Paladin howitzer is the main fire support weapon for the U.S. Army.

SPECIFICATIONS
Weight: 28.8 tonnes (31¾ tons)
Crew: 4
Width: 3.15 m (10 feet 4 inches)
Height: 3.6 m (12 feet)
Main armament: 155 mm
    howitzer

PzH2000

The German PzH2000 is a super-powerful self-propelled gun.

SPECIFICATIONS
Weight: 55.8 tonnes
    (61½ tons)
Crew: 5
Width: 3.58 m (11¾ feet)
Height: 3.06 m (10 feet)
Main armament:
    155 mm gun

HOWITZER: A short cannon that fires shells in a high arc.

BTR-90

SPECIFICATIONS
Weight: 20.9 tonnes (23 tons)
Crew: 3
Width: 3.2 m (10½ feet)
Height: 2.98 m (9¾ feet)
Main armament: 30 mm
    cannon

The AFV BTR-90 is a Russian armoured personnel carrier. There are many different models, including rocket launchers and self-propelled guns.

CHALLENGER 2

SPECIFICATIONS
Weight: 62.5 tonnes (69 tons)
Crew: 4
Width: 3.51 m (11½ feet)
Height: 2.49 m (8¼ feet)
Main armament: 120 mm
    rifled gun

The Challenger 2 is Britain's advanced main battle tank. It claims to be the most reliable MBT in the world.

SELF-PROPELLED GUN: A lightly armoured AFV with wheels or tracks.

GALLERY

T-90

The T-90 is Russia's most advanced main battle tank. It uses thermal sights to locate targets.

SPECIFICATIONS
Weight: 47.5 tonnes (52½ tons)
Crew: 3
Width: 3.78 m (12½ feet)
Height: 2.2 m (7¼ feet)
Main armament: 125 mm
  smoothbore gun

PUMA

This German IFV is well armoured and comfortable: it even has air conditioning.

SPECIFICATIONS
Weight: 31.5 tonnes
  (34¾ tons)
Crew: 3
Width: 3.6 m (12 feet)
Height: 3.6 m (12 feet)
Main armament: 30 mm
  autocannon

IFV: Infantry fighting vehicle, designed to fight with soldiers onboard.

M113A3

SPECIFICATIONS
Weight: 12.1 tonnes
(13¼ tons)
Crew: 2
Width: 2.69 m (8¾ feet)
Height: 2.5 m (8 feet)
Main armament: M2
Browning machine gun

This U.S. APC has been used in all major conflicts since the 1960s. It was named the most significant infantry vehicle of all time.

STRYKER

SPECIFICATIONS
Weight: 16.5 tonnes (18 tons)
Crew: 2
Width: 2.72 m (9 feet)
Height: 2.64 m (8 feet 8 inches)
Main armament: M2 machine gun

This APC can be transported by air to combat zones. Its armour is able to withstand roadside explosive devices.

APC: Armoured personnel carrier, used to transport troops in safety.

GLOSSARY

AFV Armoured fighting vehicle; tanks are a type of AFV.

Allied Relating to the countries that fought Germany in World War II, led by the United States, Britain and the Soviet Union.

amphibious A vehicle that works on land and in water.

APC Armoured personnel carrier, used to transport troops in safety.

Blitzkrieg A German tactic that relied on rapid advances by tanks.

cannon A powerful gun that fires heavy shells.

caterpillar tracks Metal plates joined in a continuous loop.

ceramic A strong modern material based on fired clay.

chain gun A machine-gun powered by a chain driven by a motor.

chassis The base of a vehicle that is attached to the wheels or tracks.

coalition A temporary alliance of people or countries.

fire control system Keeps the main gun locked on its target.

Golan Heights A high, flat area on the border of Syria and Israel.

howitzer A short cannon that fires shells in a high arc.

hull The main body of a tank, beneath the turret.

IFV Infantry fighting vehicle, designed to fight with soldiers onboard.

infantry Soldiers who fight on foot.

infrared A system that 'sees' objects by the radiation they give off.

main battle tank (MBT) A tank that is heavy, but still highly mobile.

NATO North Atlantic Treaty Organisation; an alliance of European and American countries.

rifled cannon A gun with grooves inside the barrel to spin a shell.

self-propelled gun A lightly armoured AFV with wheels or tracks.

shell An explosive missile or bomb.

strategic Related to the overall plan for a campaign or war.

tactics How troops and weapons are used together in warfare.

tanker A member of a tank crew.

terrain The physical shape of the land.

thermal imaging Making a picture from the heat something gives off.

Tiger German heavy tank developed in 1942 to fight Allied AFVs.

TOW Tube-launched, optically-tracked, wire-guided missile.

traction The amount of grip that pulls a vehicle along.

turret The top section of a tank; it can turn in all directions.

FURTHER READING

BOOKS

Bodden, Valerie, *Tanks* (Built for Battle). Creative Education, 2012.

Braulick, Carrie A. *U.S. Army Tanks* (Blazers Military Vehicles). Capstone Press, 2006.

Brook, Henry. *Tanks*. Usborne Publishing Ltd, 2011.

Colson, Rob Scott. *Ultimate Machines: Tanks and Military Vehicles.* Wayland, 2013.

Cornish, Geoff. *Tanks*. Military Hardware in Action). Lerner Publishing Group, 2003

Graham, Ian. *Tanks* (World's Greatest). Raintree, 2005.

Jackson, Robert. *101 Great Tanks* (101 Greatest Weapons of All Time). Rosen Publishing Group, 2010.

WEBSITES

http://www.historylearningsite. co.uk/tanks_and_world_war_one.htm
A History Learning Site page about the development of tanks during World War I.

https://science.howstuffworks.com/ m1-tank.htm
How Stuff Works page on the M1.

www.tankmuseum.com
The museum of the British Royal Tank Regiment and Royal Armoured Corps.

battletanks.com
Photographs and statistics of battle tanks since World War II.

INDEX